the **americas**

ADVISORY BOARD
Irene Vilar, series editor

also in **the americas** series

PERLA SUEZ

DREAMING of the DELTA

TRANSLATED BY RHONDA DAHL BUCHANAN

TEXAS TECH UNIVERSITY PRESS

This book is typeset in Optima. The paper used in this book meets the minimum requirements of ANSI/NISO Z39.48-1992 (R1997). ∞

Designed by Ashley Beck
Cover photograph/illustration by Perla Suez

Library of Congress Cataloging-in-Publication Data
Suez, Perla.
   [Pasajera. English]
   Dreaming of the delta / Perla Suez ; [translated by] Rhonda Dahl Buchanan.
      pages cm. — (The Americas series)
      Summary: "Argentine novel set during the Proceso de reorganización nacional; an experimental thriller that focuses on secrecy, betrayal, and violence and reflects the national struggle for power and control through the servants in a mansion in the Entre Ríos region."—Provided by publisher
      ISBN 978-0-89672-898-1 (pbk.) — ISBN 978-0-89672-899-8 (e-book)
   1. Argentina—Politics and government—1955-1983—Fiction. 2. Violence—Argentina—History—20th century—Fiction. I. Buchanan, Rhonda Lee Dahl, translator. II. Title.
      PQ7798.29.U36P3813 2015
      863'.64—dc23   2014033083

14 15 16 17 18 19 20 21 22 / 9 8 7 6 5 4 3 2 1

Texas Tech University Press
Box 41037 | Lubbock, Texas 79409-1037 USA
800.832.4042 | ttup@ttu.edu | www.ttupress.org

Work published within the framework of "SUR" Translation Support Program of the Ministry of Foreign Affairs, International Trade and Worship of the Argentine Republic.

Translator's Acknowledgments: I am grateful for the support of the University of Louisville, which enabled me to consult with the author in Argentina. I would like to express by sincere appreciation to Perla Suez for her assistance and friendship.

Interior photos by André Kertész "Touraine" and "Chez Mondrian." Photos located in the Museum Boijmans Van Beuningen in Amsterdam.

CONTENTS

The river was timeless, unending···
All was born from it, or came to it···

Juan L. Ortiz

In *Dreaming of the Delta* (*La pasajera*, 2008), Perla Suez spins a tale of secrecy and betrayal in which violence takes center stage. This private drama unfolds in a mansion on the banks of the Paraná River, while a collective tragedy erupts outside its doors. Violence is a pervasive element throughout Suez's narrative fiction, from *Memorias de Vladimir* (*Memoirs of Vladimir*, 1992), her first novel written for children, to her most recent novel, *Humo rojo* (*Red Smoke*, 2012). Although pivotal moments in Argentina's history often serve as an allusive backdrop for Suez's intimate tales, she rejects the detailed realism that characterizes the historical novel, opting instead for a stark minimalist prose that resembles the evocative lines of poetry, and invites her readers to fill the blank spaces of the page with their own interpretations.

In her previous novels, which comprise *The Entre Ríos Trilogy* (2006), Suez incorporates significant events that are crucial to the formation of national identity while keeping her lens focused on the traumatic moments that determine the psychological development of her adolescent characters. As the title of the trilogy suggests, the action of these three novels takes place in the Entre Ríos province, where the author spent the first fifteen years of her life. Perla Yagupsky Suez is the granddaughter of Ashkenazi Jews who fled the pogroms of Czar Nicholas II at the end of the nineteenth century and sought refuge in the agricultural colonies of Entre Ríos, an area designated as a new Zion by Baron Maurice de Hirsch, founder of the Jewish Colonization Association. Suez grew up listening to her father and grandfather spin tales of adventure, passion, intolerance, and repression from the Old World and their adopted homeland. Years later, details of these migratory experiences would find their way into her fiction, and just as her grandparents emigrated from Russia in 1889 to escape the persecution of Jews, so too the author would escape the perils of the military dictatorship by embarking on a journey of exile to France in 1977.

Dreaming of the Delta represents a departure from Suez's previous novels in that none of the characters are members of the Jewish community, nor are they adolescents; nevertheless, several elements remain constant: the journey, violence, memory, the search for identity and belonging, and the insertion of decisive moments in Argentine history into a story that takes place in the province of Entre Ríos, along the shores of the river of her childhood memories. In this novel and her other works, Suez reveals the storms that brew in the seemingly quiet lives of her humble characters, who turn out to be not-so-common folk. After nearly fifty years of serving the Admiral and his wife in their stately mansion, Tránsito, their sixty-seven-year-old maid, decides the time has finally come to return to the islands of her childhood in the Paraná River Delta, but not before unleashing decades of silent resentment in a fatal act of vengeance.

Like the timeless river of the Entre Ríos province, from which all things come and all things go, Suez's words ebb and flow across the pages of this novel, leaving in their wake volatile voids that suggest to the reader that what is not disclosed is as powerful as what is revealed. With a skeletal prose that is deceptively austere and transparent, the author condenses decades of cruelty and longing into a few brief hours that transpire after the funeral of the Admiral. Blurring the line between novel, theater, and film, the author structures her tale into a dramatic work in three acts, each featuring the voice of one of the Admiral's three servants. The cast of characters appears at the end of the novel, as it would in a film: Tránsito the Servant; her younger sister, Lucía the Cook; Ortiz the Chauffeur; and the Señora, the Admiral's wife, whose voice is silenced soon after her husband is buried.

In this novel, which resembles a screenplay or theatrical script, Suez employs an experimental style of writing that emphasizes the important role of visual imagery. Dialogue, indicated in italics in the original novel, is the primary tool used to disclose significant information about the characters; however, at times it is a challenge for the reader to determine who is speaking or if the characters are expressing their unspoken thoughts or simply thinking out loud. When the omniscient narrator intervenes, it is often to provide stage instructions, like a playwright indicating the blocking of the actors' movements. The narration calls for active participation on the part of the reader, who must be aware that certain scenes will be replayed with slight differences, depending on who is speaking or remembering the moment. Like fitting the pieces of a puzzle together, eventually the reader will create order out of the nonchronological units of text and ultimately will discover that some elements of the plot remain intentionally unresolved.

Although memories and dreams occupy more narrative space in this novel than dramatic action, the two violent acts that serve as catalysts for the plot are riveting. When the Admiral is writhing in pain on his deathbed, Tránsito does not hesitate to administer two vials of tranquilizer, instead of one, to put an end to his misery. Soon after returning from the funeral, she commits a second act of homicide when she smothers the Admiral's wife with a pillow rather than serving her the glass of orange juice she had requested.

The reader is left to wonder about the motives behind both homicides. Those who could provide the answers are no longer alive, and the author leaves few clues in her bare-bones account of the crimes. With nothing standing in her way, Tránsito prepares herself for the final journey to her childhood home: the idyllic islands of the Delta. She had always believed that her sister would accompany her, but Lucía informs her that she and Ortiz have bought the last plots available in the new section of the cemetery, a purchase that will unite them beyond death. What Tránsito does not know is that Lucía has also made a promise to her mother to never reveal the secret of her sister's birth. While Tránsito cherishes the myth of her origins that her mother told her as a child, that she gave birth to her in a canoe in the middle of the Paraná river, Lucía knows the truth, that while cleaning the bathroom of the Pueblo Brugo bus station early one morning, her mother rescued a bloody newborn from the floor, minutes after a passenger "in transit" boarded a bus headed for the border, abandoning her baby forever. Without her sister to accompany her, Tránsito decides to take the Señora with her on the journey home, but not before taking the time to savor a few moments of absolute control. Prior to leaving the house, Tránsito delivers a series of monologues to her dead mistress, filled with elements of violence and black humor reminiscent of a script for the Theater of the Absurd or the Theater of Cruelty.

For years, Suez resisted the idea of writing a novel set during the dictatorship of 1976–1983, recognizing the challenges of representing in fiction the cruel reality of the period designated by the military junta as *El Proceso de Reorganización Nacional*, the National Reorganization Process, or simply *El Proceso*. In *Dreaming of the Delta*, Suez creates scenes that convey the legacy of silence, which marked the darkest chapter in Argentina's history, by employing the art of allusion and a deceptively sparse prose whose incisive words are capable of drawing blood like a paper cut. A simple gesture, an evocative photograph, the appearance of ellipsis within sentences, wide margins between paragraphs, and vast blank spaces on the page suggest to the reader that silence can be as revealing and powerful as the written or spoken word. The author makes a conscious effort not to give her readers a history lesson, allowing the highly charged empty spaces on the page to suggest what is too traumatic to reveal in explicit terms.

Significant allusions to the Argentine dictatorship are minimal. Ortiz the Chauffeur dutifully shines the Admiral's car, a Ford Falcon, but nowhere in the novel is it explained that green Ford Falcons were the vehicles provided to the military for their operations, nor is the color of the car mentioned. It is also known that during the dictatorship newborn infants were stolen from women who gave birth in detention centers and clandestine camps, but in the novel Tránsito only makes a vague insinuation to the black-market adoptions in a comment to the Admiral's wife: "You couldn't even give him a son. Just as well you refused to adopt that baby boy he managed to get for you." Perhaps the most blatant reference to the *Proceso* period is the placement of the date, April 7, 1979, as the title for the final act of the novel. This epilogue is narrated by Ortiz the Chauffeur, who recollects a trip he made with the Admiral to the Chilean border, shortly before his *patrón* contracted a fatal illness. For the first time, through the recesses of Ortiz's memory, the reader hears the Admiral's voice when he responds to his chauffeur's request that they cross the border: "The road to the border is mined. We're going to smash those sons of bitches! If they want war, that's what we're going to give them. The islands and the Beagle belong to us. Those shitty Chileans will see what we Argentines are made of." The Admiral's response provides a glimpse into the bitter conflict between Argentina and Chile over the Beagle Channel, which nearly brought the two countries to the brink of war in 1978.

Although the atrocities of the dictatorship drew sharp criticism, none of them seem to be of any concern to Tránsito and her sister Lucía, whose insular existence is determined by the same domestic routines of servitude that they have performed daily since arriving at the mansion from the islands of the Paraná Delta, nearly fifty years ago, when Tránsito was seventeen years old and Lucía, twelve. Nevertheless, the personal drama that plays out under the roof of the Admiral's house mirrors in many ways the national tragedy. The mansion is a house divided by class struggle and racial prejudice, by abundance and deprivation, by those who have what others can only dream of possessing, all symbolized by the image of a staircase that separates the world of the servants from that of the masters. In this asphyxiating climate of repressed desires, intolerance, secrets, and pent-up resentment, Tránsito's promise to her mother to return to the islands of the Delta, the only place where she feels she belongs, sustains her and determines her actions. After years of servitude in a house that was never her home, Tránsito begins a journey to find a place where she belongs, a journey that now awaits the reader as well.

Rhonda Dahl Buchanan

DREAMING of the DELTA

ACT 1

The old woman who walks at a steady, brisk pace with her head held high is sixty-seven years old and belongs to a world that no longer exists. She is tall and thin and wears her hair short. In one hand she carries a bag, and in the other, her purse. She looks down the deserted street and heads toward the river.

The sky is white, the cobblestone path wet. A strange calm envelops the shore.

The old woman stops, hesitates, and looks at some gourds that are hanging from the branches of a ceibo tree and swaying in the wind.

She heads to the wharf, where the ferries that take passengers to the islands are moored.

She has time to spare.

My name is Tránsito. I turned sixty-seven last month, and I am the one the Señora relied on to run her house for more than forty years. Her husband had their mansion built on a high bluff, near the banks. You can see the river from there.

Not long ago, we returned from the funeral of my *patrón*, but I can still hear the sound of his footsteps as if he were here. I see him in his uniform, gaunt, those beady eyes of his not missing a thing. The scent of funeral flowers lingers in the air.

I can't sit still. I walk around the house with a weight on my chest as heavy as a rock. I go back and forth but can't find a thing to do. Something's buzzing in my ears. The walls are cold and the floors creak. The worst is over: the Señor died.

The Señora's resting in her room. It's been years since she left the house, but today she had no choice.

The house is isolated. The owners brought the plans from Europe, copied from a *château* they saw in Southern France. The Gobelin tapestries, the *chaise longue,* the soft *bergère* chair, and other furniture, all arrived by boat. In the garden, the Carrara marble fountain, filled with goldfish, came from Italy.

My sister, Lucía, lives with me and is a good cook, tidy and careful. Over the years, she has learned to move lightly, without making a sound. At times, it's impossible to know what she's thinking. She has her own way of seeing things. She doesn't complicate her life or worry about what may happen. I wish I were that way, but I'm not. I can't settle for less; I want something more for myself.

Back when we lived on the island, a tick bit her, and that's why she has heart problems and sometimes walks around in a daze. Ever since then, I shudder to think she might die. There are no ticks in the Delta now, so they say.

We have to be ready for the day when one of us is no longer here. I've spent so many years by her side, worrying myself sick over her health, with what's to become of me if she dies. Where will I go without Lucía? Who knows? For the longest time, I've been living in fear that death is waiting to take her away from me.

Tránsito goes into the kitchen and says to the cook, *I'm thirsty.*

Lucía gets a glass, fills it with water from the tap, and places it on the table.

The old woman gulps down the water and then breathes a sigh of relief. She sits down with her back to her sister and gazes through the open kitchen door at the garden's marble fountain, surrounded by cypress trees, and says to her,

I had a dream, Sister.

Lucía listens as she rinses the rice.

We were playing with Beatriz in the woods behind our cabin, and I saw you whisper something in her ear. Your face was not your face, and Beatriz looked at me wide-eyed and covered her mouth, and you laughed. I asked you to tell me the secret too, but you said no, and the two of you ran away.

Tránsito rises and tells her sister she has to get back to the Señora.

Lucía asks her,

Do you want me to stay with her for a while?

If I need you, I'll call you.

The old woman walks out of the kitchen. Lucía turns, watches her leave, and remembers that afternoon when they were playing behind their cabin and she whispered in Beatriz's ear something she promised her mother never to repeat.

Tránsito opens the bedroom door and enters with a tray in her hands. The Señora is lying in bed, face up, with her eyes closed. She orders her in a hoarse voice to leave the pill and orange juice on the nightstand and to close the door on her way out.

The servant hears a muffled drone striking her ears and pounces on the Señora, covering her head with a pillow and smothering her face. The Señora kicks and groans, fighting with her hands and fingernails.

Tránsito hears nothing. She thinks of nothing. She gathers all her strength into her arms and keeps pushing the pillow, pressing until the body goes limp and remains still. The Señora's bones and muscles surrender slowly. Tránsito removes the pillow and sees that the *patrona*'s eyes are open, her mouth as well, as if she were about to say something. One of her arms dangles, nearly touching the floor.

The servant props her up against the headboard and murmurs,

I had a hard time shutting you up.

She lines up the dead woman's slippers at the foot of the bed and leaves.

She goes downstairs to the dining room and takes out a *Para ti* from the magazine stand and sits down and leafs through it. Her eyes feel heavy, and as she closes them, for a moment, it seems as if she is no longer in the armchair.

The Señor commanded a fleet of ships, but died alone like a dog. Near the end, he barely weighed seventy pounds. They say you go out the way you came in and that leaving takes only an instant. I'm not so sure about that; perhaps you can go back another way.

The Señora put me in charge of caring for the *patrón*, and that was more than I could handle. I thought it was too hard for an old woman like me to look after a dying man. I couldn't take it anymore and begged God to just let him die, but he kept hanging on.

I woke up with my mouth dry, sitting in the armchair in the dining room, the *Para ti* in my hands, and from that portrait, hanging on the wall, I saw the Señor and the Señora and all of their family staring at me.

I felt ashamed.

I'm leaving everything in order. I don't owe a thing.
I'm finally going to escape from this prison.

I should get my hair cut and these roots dyed. I can't go back looking like this.

A little later, the old woman goes out the front door and walks down the cobblestone path toward the river. She heads to the pier that is about a thousand feet from the house. In one hand she carries a bag, and in the other, her purse. From her neck hang the keys to the house and a small gray flannel bag.

She keeps walking until she comes to the wharf where the ferryboats to the islands are docked. She steps right up to the ticket window, thinking that she can finally decide what to do. She opens her purse and takes out some money, but as she goes to pay for the ticket, she has second thoughts and returns to the house.

On the way back, Tránsito recalls that moment during the Señor's funeral when they were closing the casket and the Señora, standing at the edge of the grave, cried for them to bury her with him, and as she tried to calm the *patrona* down, the thought crossed her mind that there was no point in the Señora making such a fuss because she was already buried in her own house.

For some time, Tránsito had lost patience with the Señora. For some time, the servant had wanted to tell her things she never would have said before. She should have looked for another job a long time ago. She had thought about it more than once, but did not have the courage and stayed.

She regrets nothing. She did everything for her bosses, until the Señor fell ill, and she realized everyone in that house was old. After that, nothing was the same. It was overwhelming.

Tránsito enters through the service door, hides the bag in the cabinet where they store the cylinders of gas, and looks around. No one sees her. Ortiz, the chauffeur, is shining the Señor's car, as if he were going to take him somewhere. Lucía is in the kitchen drying the coffee cups from the wake.

Neither of them speaks to her as she passes by, nor does she utter a word.

The servant climbs the stairs, opens the bedroom door, takes a few steps, and looks at the dead woman with rage, shaking her finger at her,

What do you want from me now, you old bitch! What do you need me for?

Why are you sneering with that old scowl of yours, like you smell shit?

You still want to see something? There's nothing more to see. There's no more time to waste sewing or looking at patterns.

You lived seventy-five years, you shouldn't complain. Not everyone's that lucky. You spent seventy-five years yacking away, and I finally shut you up.

You were born with a silver spoon in your mouth, so you never had to suffer. Think about how you spent your time, Señora, and you'll see I'm right.

You didn't give a damn that he had another woman in Oro Verde.

I'll tell you something else: you're cold, as frigid as ice inside. In fact, you only married the patrón *for his money. What do you need so much dough for anyway, tell me?*

The servant leans over the dead woman and says as she lowers her eyelids,

Stop your grumbling.

Anyway, you've been sprawled out on that bed like a cow for a decade.

I'm the one who took care of this house. You were lucky to have me, but I can't say the same about you.

Tránsito goes over to the dresser and opens each drawer, one by one. Nothing new. She rummages through everything, as usual, takes out the Señor's wallet and sees money inside. She counts the bills and then stashes them in her brassiere.

She turns and sees on the Señora's hand the white gold emerald ring that belonged to her mother-in-law. The servant removes it from the *patrona*'s finger and puts it in the small grey flannel bag hanging from her neck.

The Señora's knitting lies on the armchair: one of the two sleeves she was knitting for a jacket. The servant sets aside the knitting, drags the armchair to the dead woman's bed, sits down, and continues speaking,

It's too late for regrets. You killed him.

And tell me, what did you get out of it? What, you old bitch?

The patrón *put up with you because he was patient. A great man, who'd gone to war, caring for you in his house like a fool. What did he see in a mule like you? You couldn't even give him a son. Just as well you refused to adopt that baby boy he managed to get for you.*

We were the only ones who cared for the Señor until the very end, Lucía, Ortiz, and I. You managed to wriggle your way out of that. You don't abandon a dying man, and that's exactly what you did. Aren't you ashamed of yourself?

The Señor hoped he'd survive, even though he was wasting away to nothing at the end. And even though he didn't want to go and he knew no one could save him, he died anyway.

At the end, he'd scream in pain all night long until he'd lose his voice. I took care of him every day. He didn't want to eat, and every day he'd piss and shit all over himself. That's why I didn't hesitate for a moment when I had to help him yesterday. I changed the I.V. and gave him two vials of sedative instead of one.

He sighed, Oh, Tránsito.

He barely complained and fell right to sleep.

Soon his heart stopped.

And you, as selfish as you are, worried about not getting enough rest.

Now you can rest all you want.

Tránsito stands up, leans over the dead woman, opens her mouth, and yanks out her false teeth. She puts them in her pocket and leaves the room.

She hurries down the stairs, crosses the patio, and walks to the garden. She sticks her hand in her pocket, takes something out, and throws it into the fountain. At that moment, the cook sees her,

What did you throw in there?

Crumbs for the fish.

You're going to kill them.

Quit following me.

Then Tránsito makes something up about the Señora losing her handkerchief when she got out of the car, after returning from the cemetery, and says they need to look for it. Lucía assures her they would have seen it by now, and that if she lost it getting out of the car, the wind would have blown it away.

Tránsito tells her sister to look for it along the shore, and meanwhile, runs back to the fountain and sees the Señora's false teeth in the bottom. She sticks her hand in the water and fishes them out, rubbing them on her dress to dry them, and then puts them back in her pocket.

Lucía follows Tránsito and enters the bedroom behind her without being seen.

Pardon me, Señora, for bothering you. I looked for it too, but your handkerchief's no where to be found.

Tránsito hears her, grabs her by the arm, and shoves her into the hallway, shouting,

I already found it. Have Ortiz take you to buy aspirin for the Señora!

When she gets rid of Lucía, Tránsito locks the door and walks over to the bed again,

Open wide, Señora!

She tries to put the false teeth back in place, but cannot.

Close your mouth. Can't you see they're going to fall out, and this time I'm not going to run and find them for you.

Exhausted, Tránsito sits down again in the armchair and rests quietly. She closes her eyes for a moment, but suddenly opens them, jumps up, and keeps talking to her,

Tell me, when did you begin to mistrust me and think I was stealing? That night money disappeared from the house and you called me a thief?

Me, of all people, the one who took care of everything and never forgot that you were the patrona *and I was the servant.*

The problem is that you have the brains of a bird. Do you remember when you pounded your fist on the table and accused me of stealing that silk handkerchief? I remember it very well. And now you go and tell me to look for it, because you dropped it getting out of the car, after returning from the cemetery. I've had it!

Why did you think I was the one who had rifled through your friend Finita's purse? You think we islanders can't be trusted, don't you? Bullshit. I'll never forgive you for that. I don't deserve being insulted like that.

You knew me; we lived together for so many years.

No matter how upset you were over the Señor's illness, I won't forgive you.

I swear to you I had to pull myself together, swallow my pride, and move on. That was the first time I thought about leaving, going somewhere else.

But where? And what would I do?

The phone on the nightstand rings.

The servant answers and hears the voice of a man at the other end of the line. He identifies himself as Major Arruaba-rrena and asks for the Señora.

Speaking. A pleasure, Major.

Thank you.

Yes, he was a great man.

A good companion.

Thank you very much. Good-bye.

Instead of hanging up, Tránsito rests the receiver on her lap and shouts,

Don't play the saint with me, Señora! You were rifling through my things and I caught you and told you, look who's calling the kettle black . . .

I don't think another servant would have put up with crap like that!

I'll never forget that afternoon when you came into the patrón's bedroom. By then he was going downhill, and I heard you, Señora, asking him where he kept his mother's white gold ring. You'd do whatever it took to get him to tell you where he kept that emerald ring, as if you were afraid he'd take it with him to the grave.

The servant sits there, with the receiver on her lap, thinking,

When it comes down to it, I came with the clothes on my back from a forsaken place in the world, and I managed to earn a living and then some. ·

I have a place to return to, like Mother wished.

There are many places on the island, and once I'm there, I'll choose one. I'd rather be buried in an urn, like Grandmother, seated with my elbows on my knees, my face between my hands, shrouded in a woolen cloth.

No one can make me leave. No one.

Yes, Señora. That's right. You heard what I'm telling you, even though you don't like it.

The servant rubs her hands together, feeling cold, even though the room is warm. She looks for a peppermint, the Señora's favorite candy, puts one in her mouth, and sucks on it noisily while keeping an eye on the *patrona*.

Now you went and gave me your cold and made me sick. That's all I need now, to catch pneumonia because of you . . . I've got this damn cough that I can't shake.

I wasn't sick a day in my life, except once when I had the measles, and even then I still had to take care of Lucía. I had to help Mother.

You, on the other hand, always complaining about one thing or another. You liked everyone to feel sorry for you, and I just can't stand that.

That's why I say you must be blind to call me worthless and scream at me that I was out of my mind to keep taking care of the Señor. The one who was losing her marbles was you, you old witch, because like I told you already, you have the brains of a bird, you hear me?

Let me tell you there are more important things than wasting time playing cards, sitting there like you're watching the river go by.

It's so hard to understand you people when you talk to each other. We have to be careful because you smile when you're enjoying yourselves and when you're giving orders, so we never know what you're really thinking.

I'm not going to stay tied to you inside this place. No. Your house isn't the same anymore. It seems like a crypt, a tomb for four old people.

I got tired of taking care of your things as if they were mine, fed up . . .

Before I leave, I want to remind you there's still something here I'm going to take with me, so get ready.

Tránsito wishes she could sit down a while but she cannot. She looks for the Señora's knitting she had thrown on the floor, picks it up, examines it, and says to her,

How many times did I tell you it would turn out nicer if you used angora wool and jersey stitch? But no, you were born too high and mighty to listen to anyone.

An unbearable noise pounds in her ears, and she drops the knitting onto the floor.

Tránsito sees the glass of orange juice she brought the Señora a while ago and gulps it down. She remembers, without knowing why, that day her brother was born, and once again she sees her mother lying quietly on the cot. Beetles scurry over the dirt floor of the cabin and her mother tells her to disinfect it with Creolin.

Outside someone is singing,

Guarumbo Taito, Guarumbo Ahuevé, échale caá, toma tereré, échale caá, échale caá, échale caá . . .

The old woman does not understand why she feels a weight on her chest and a bitter taste in her mouth.

When I first came to work in this big house, I was seventeen years old, shy, and embarrassed by everything. I was
always afraid and my hands would sweat. The slightest thing
embarrassed me. I felt ashamed when I ate or when I walked
down those long hallways. It didn't seem right for me to go
upstairs or to have my own room.

But the worse thing was speaking, opening my mouth. I
barely managed to nod my head. At school, I'd hide like an
ostrich.

It would take more than forty years of waiting on others for
me to start taking care of myself and to realize that not even
the room I thought was mine, belonged to me.

A lush and gentle rain was falling when Mother was giving birth to my brother. My stepfather, Lucía, and I waited outside the cabin under a tent so we wouldn't get wet.

The door opened, and the midwife came out and told us that my brother had been born with blue blood and that he might not live.

We went in, and I saw Mother, pale, lying on the cot. At that moment, I heard a gasp escape from my brother's throat, and I forced his mouth open so he could breathe.

My stepfather looked at him without saying a word and then glared at Mother with a scowl on his face and said that couldn't be his son because blue blood didn't run in his veins. He said that purple thing Mother had given birth to was a combination of all the men she'd ever slept with.

He left the cabin in a rage, and I followed him. As he headed toward the river, I realized my stepfather wasn't drunk that day.

As time passed, I grew a little more fond of Lucía's father, because while he was with us, he treated me as if I were his daughter too.

But then he left.

Tránsito takes the Señora's knitting and starts making a ball, unraveling one sleeve, then the other, as she mumbles,

Soon I'm going to paddle up the wide river in a canoe, gazing at my face in the water until I reach that place, past the canal, where Mother told me she gave birth to me.

Mother always used to tell me that I should never forget to come back. But why do you care about that? You never even asked me about her.

I owe it to myself to go back to the islands, and besides, I like the idea of not having to listen to that good-for-nothing and that everything will be as simple as when I was a little girl and caught a catfish with my bare hand and Lucía cheered for me.

The servant runs her finger over the nightstand, resigned that she will have to dust it again. At that moment, someone knocks on the door.

Tránsito orders,

Don't you move, Señora.

She tosses the ball of yarn under the bed and goes to open the door.

Lucía is there with a telegram in her hands.

Tránsito says to her,

Not you again, what do you want?

Another message of condolence arrived.

Give it to me.

No, I want to give it to her myself.

Better to do that at dinner.

Lucía stands there waiting.

What are you waiting for?

The cook looks at her and says,

I don't think it's right that you order the patrona *around. I heard you!*

You're not going to tell me how I should treat her.

The cook turns and leaves.

The last thing I need is for an old biddy like you to order me around!

My brother was only a few months old when he died. We paddled the canoe along the ravine until we came to a slope low enough to climb with the coffin. We buried him in the woods among the *tala* and *espinillo* trees, and then Mother, Lucía, and I sat in the boat, near the grave, and wept until dusk fell.

Tránsito hears her sister's footsteps fading away. She goes to the armoire, opens the door, and takes out the Señora's fur coat. She wraps herself up in it and smiles with a childish look on her face. She gazes at herself from head to toe in the mirror and plays with the ermine's paws, then spins around,

Look at me, not too long or too short. It fits me just right, just the way I like it. As well as it fit you. You lied when you told me that white made me look darker. It's a good thing I was on to you.

You remember, not long ago, it was my birthday, and you said you wanted to give me an angora coat, but you ended up buying me that jacket that got tiny balls all over it the first Sunday I wore it.

People like you never change.

More than once you thought about replacing me with a younger woman, but you didn't have the nerve to bring a new girl here.

And to think that this morning I was by your side at the Señor's funeral and gave you a hug and my condolences. Life is strange, Señora, nothing happens to us like we hope it will and that's just the way it is, life has its secrets, and you have to respect them.

Just then the servant remembers the strange way the Señor looked at her the day she arrived at the house with Lucía, after traveling by boat from the nameless islands to the city.

They had been left orphans and arrived with only the clothes on their backs. In that house, they were given a place to live, hot food, and their own rooms. Their masters bought for them shoes and notebooks and made sure they finished school. They were taught good manners and they felt protected, which is worth something.

At first, as naïve as I was, I took care of everything like I was working in a castle. Both my sister and I went to great pains to do everything as best we could.

For me, deep down, the only thing that mattered ever since my sister was born, was for her to be healthy and happy and for my masters to appreciate and trust me.

I'm a fool, I get too attached to things . . . I'm going to miss watching television with the Señora.

At night, after all the work was done, I'd lie in bed, face up, staring into the darkness without moving, until one time Lucía asked me what was wrong.

I want to go back, I told her.

We can't.

I gave in and kept myself busy. I wasn't alone; Lucía was there.

The servant descends the stairs slowly, wearing the coat. She saunters down the long hallway toward her room. She hears no footsteps, not a sound. Nothing. No one.

She opens the armoire and takes out nail polish and remover, then returns to the Señora,

Just to show you that I'm not resentful, I'm going to paint your nails before I leave. Compared to my hands, yours are prettier and whiter. Probably because they never did a day's work.

I brought the polish and the remover. They're mine, but I'll let you borrow them. It'll just take a minute.

The old woman paints one of the *patrona*'s hands but forgets the other one. She leaves the bottles on the dresser and stares out the window at the Carrara marble fountain in the garden. She likes how the water spills out of the lion's mouth.

Then, she turns around.

The armoire and bed are the same and where they have always been. The green rug that the servant swept so many times still covers the floor. The small table and the lamp are where they belong, but she sees everything differently.

Silence and tranquility settle over that big house, but the old woman feels an emptiness within and a strange sense of urgency.

It's getting dark, and I have to go soon. I'm not sad that I'm leaving this house. My mind's made up. I have to look ahead and realize that I'm no longer here.

It's morning, the rain has stopped, and Lucía's father is walking toward the river. I follow him. I know he's not coming back. When he gets to the shore, he stops and looks at me.

Help me, Daughter.

He shoves the canoe that is stuck in the mud, floating among the bulrushes, and I help him. He gets in, puts the oars in the water, and as the canoe slowing begins to move, he waves good-bye and heads downstream.

The smell of coffee coming from the kitchen rouses her. The servant would like to have a cup before dinner. She goes to the door, opens it, wonders if she should go downstairs or not, and stands in the doorway, hesitating.

I was twenty years old . . . Ortiz introduced me to someone he knew. I went out with him, and he took me to the square. He had a kiosk in the port and made a good living. I liked that man. He was polite.

Later, he put his hand on my leg, and I removed it.

I have to go, I told him.

He looked at me with a long face, then took me back to the house, and I never saw him again.

The cook calls everyone to dinner.

The servant takes off the Señora's coat, peers out the door, and tells her,

We're coming.

She closes the door and warns,

I'm going to call Señora Finita now and she's going to find out what you did to the Señor.

At the funeral, Señora Finita said, poor Rosario, what a martyr, staying up all night taking care of him.

Some martyr!

Do you know who I am?

When I was little, I used to pretend that I was dying. Once I lay down in a coffin that had washed up on the shore, and I stayed still for a long time, lying there, beneath a tree, with my eyes closed until I fell asleep. The cry of a limpkin woke me, and I ran away scared.

The servant enters the family dining room where Ortiz and Lucía are waiting at the table.

Tránsito says,

The Señora won't be coming down. She wants peace and quiet, and she's not hungry.

Lucía says,

I'll take a cup of tea up to her later.

Look how worked up you are, Lucía, you should go to bed and let me take care of things.

Your sister's right, says Ortiz.

What about her? Just look at her, she's pale.

That's enough, you two!

They fall silent, and the chauffeur calms down and says,

We're going to miss the Señor.

Lucía and Tránsito agree.

Lucía asks,

And the Señora, how's she going to go on without him?

It won't be easy, says Ortiz.

It's just a matter of time, Tránsito adds.

The three eat in silence, and when they finish dinner, the servant gets up and clears the plates. The cook leaves, and the chauffeur follows her.

Tránsito puts her fork down before swallowing the last bite, then gets up, clears the plates from the table, and puts them in the sink under running water. The chauffeur tells her to leave them, that he will wash them, but the old woman does not let him.

Lucía and Ortiz leave, and Tránsito remains alone.

She washes the dishes and afterwards turns around and sees the Señora's plate on the table, untouched. She looks at the fork and does not know why it reminds her of the pitchfork her stepfather always leaned against the side of the cabin.

She puts the plates away and goes out on the patio. A light mist is falling as she walks.

The old woman bends down and pulls up some weeds invading the rosebushes until she feels tired, and then she walks toward the bank and looks down and sees that the canoe is tied tightly to the pier of the house.

The trunks of the weeping willows are the color of blood.

She steps lightly over the mud, stops, lifts her head, looks up at the threatening sky, and murmurs,

Help me, Mother.

ACT 2

I am Lucía. It seems as if life is passing me by. April's almost over, and even though it's still light outside, the house is dark inside.

The Señor is dead. The air is still heavy with the scent of funeral flowers.

A caravan of Army trucks and cars accompanied his remains. He was laid to rest with so many honors; they even shot off the cannons in the port. And so many wreaths were delivered. It just goes to show how well respected he was.

His enemies were there too. They waited to see him dead so they could talk about him, about the man who fulfilled his duties until his dying day.

Lucía tries to remember the Señor's face, but it escapes her. *There's nothing to remember now*, she tells herself. She searches for his face in her memory, but it has vanished. The Señor does not exist, but his uniform is still there, hanging in the armoire.

As the cook heats a kettle of water, she thinks about how fortunate she was to have had him as her *patrón*. He was a generous man to her.

My mother cleans the bathrooms in the Pueblo Brugo terminal, and I keep her company that afternoon, while Tránsito and Ortiz go to the port to sell what they can.

She sings to me,

"Zumba mamá, la rumba y tambó/mabimba, mabomba, bomba y bombó."

My arm fell asleep, she says.

Suddenly, she turns pale, leans against the wall, stumbles, and falls to the floor.

I make the coffee very strong, just the way Ortiz likes it, while Tránsito takes the Señora the orange juice she asked for.

The Señora . . . I've struggled so many years to please her, but she favors Tránsito. I'm not jealous over it, but it's not fair. I just wish she'd look me in the eye when she speaks to me.

The *patrona*'s almost always in a bad mood, with a look of disgust on her face. That's kind of how she is with everyone, but with me it's worse.

My job is to cook, and I know I do the best I can. The Señor used to say there was nothing like my stuffed grape leaves.

I'm not like other women. I don't like to bad-mouth anyone, but I have to admit, when it comes to Tránsito, I don't like the way she answers our bosses. She works as much or less than I do, but makes it seem as if she works twice as hard.

Not too long ago, the Señora paid for her to take a mail-order sewing course, and she didn't even thank her for it. That just makes my hair stand on end.

I have to find the right time to tell her what I think, but she's so difficult that the slightest thing upsets her and she starts screaming.

I realize that she tries to act like the *patrona*, and it embarrasses me that she doesn't know her place. The poor thing doesn't realize she wasn't born in the same cradle as the Señora.

Ever since my mother died, may she rest in peace, I can feel her near me whenever I want. We are together, one inside the other. It's for her sake that I put up with Tránsito, but I don't know how much longer I can stand her.

I was really little when my mother told me that if I revealed what we knew about Tránsito, she'd give me away to the gypsies.

I remember that one morning I got up the nerve and gave her a piece of my mind.

Tránsito, what makes you think you can dress like the patrona? *I'm telling you this for your own good. Don't be ridiculous. If Mother were alive, she'd have told you what I'm telling you now.*

After that, she looked at me with sad eyes, and I pretended nothing had happened.

I didn't want anything to come between us, but sometimes it's complicated. Like everyone else, deep down inside, I just want to live in peace.

The next Sunday she used her sewing course as an excuse for not going out with me. She stayed in the house the whole afternoon, sewing a dress, or cutting out patterns they sent her for the course. You should have seen her with the Señora, one white and the other dark, speaking to each other as equals, while they cut out the brown paper and marked it with chalk.

I hate cheap clothes. They end up costing twice as much work.

When it comes down to it, Tránsito wants to forget that she's from the Delta, but that's impossible. My mother raised her where it smelled of fish and roots, where there was no electricity, and we had to feed the chickens.

As for me, I carry the sound of the surging water here, in my head. The river would rise with a fury and swallow the earth, and we'd scurry so the water wouldn't carry us away. The river would get rough in the summer, then much calmer in the winter, but it never stopped. We'd hear it whenever we gathered firewood and when the ferry picked us up for school. We heard it all the time. That's how it was there, and you don't forget that.

The cook, the chauffeur, and the servant have known each other since childhood. A year after losing his wife, Ortiz asked them to come work for his bosses, who with the death of his wife, were left without help.

Over time, the cook and the chauffeur began to look at each other differently. Lucía did not want Tránsito to know about their relationship, and her sister ignored it, because she did not want to know about it either.

The three of them shared many memories, but in spite of that, they did not speak to each other about the islands or their childhood.

On rare occasions the servant would bring up the subject, but the chauffeur and the cook would cut her off and change the topic.

The hearse takes the Señora back to the house.

Lucía and Tránsito get into the Señor's car. Ortiz leaves to get help when he cannot get it started. He says he will not be long.

The servant and the cook stay behind, in the middle of nowhere, waiting for the chauffeur to return. The servant has something on her mind. The cook taps her right foot impatiently.

Lucía, calm down, they'll fix the car.

She does not respond.

The servant looks at her, wanting to say something. She thinks for a moment, then says to her,

Lucía, listen to me, now that we've buried the Señor, there's nothing here anymore. Everything ended with his death, Sister. We don't have many more years left, and we've always been together. How long are you going to keep working the way you do, with that condition of yours? At night, the only thing you want to do is fall into bed. Lucía, face it, you can hardly breathe. One of these days, you won't be able to get up.

It's time to go back to the Delta. I've given it a lot of thought, and we shouldn't put it off. After all, we have our savings and with that we can fix up the cabin and stop living off other people. That money belongs to us as much as we belong to the islands.

There is no response.

Tell me what you're thinking, Lucía!

Lucía hears her, but does not look at her.

It is early morning.

A passenger comes out of the restroom at the Pueblo Brugo terminal. She cannot be more than twenty years old and walks along the platform with faltering steps, lost in thought. She gets on the bus headed for the border and leaves in it.

It's not true that Tránsito was born in a canoe on the way to Pueblo Brugo, as she believes. My mother found her abandoned, covered in blood on the bathroom floor, early one morning while she was working at the terminal. She gave her a nipple and sugary water trickled out. Then she took off her slip and wrapped her in it and continued working, without saying a word.

No one asked her a thing.

Five years later, I was born from her womb, and Tránsito helped her raise me.

Lucía is worn out, with barely enough strength to carry on, and does not want to hear anymore about Tránsito's plans.

Everywhere you look, the house is falling apart, Sister. It's falling apart slowly but surely, Lucía. Can't you see that? We have to go back where we belong.

Lucía responds,

The house is not falling apart, and it will not fall apart, and this is not the time to talk about that. For God's sake, Tránsito, let's change the subject!

Tránsito does not let up,

We have to cross to the other side, and even though we leave behind our life here, I want us to return together. I promised Mother that I was never going to abandon you.

Tránsito couldn't bear to know she was abandoned. She's a nervous person, and on top of that, ever since she was little, she likes to exaggerate things. I can just see her drowning herself in the river, and it would be all my fault. I'd never forgive myself for that.

When I see her scrubbing away, she reminds me of Mother cleaning the bathrooms in the bus terminal. Tránsito scrubs the hallway and stairs on her knees, and spends hours and days cleaning the floors, moving her arms as she sweeps the broom over the tiles. She bends down with her head very low and her ass high in the air.

But Mother wasn't like that . . . She knew her place and was always content.

Lucía remembers the afternoons when she, Ortiz, and Trán-sito would sell pastries to the passengers who crossed the river by ferry to the islands.

Ortiz dreamed about driving one of those big trucks that made long hauls. He liked to watch them get loaded onto the barges at the dock. She was eight years old and he nineteen, and she thought of him as a grown man.

Suddenly, my father started to come home drunk and would insult my mother while she washed the sheets in silence, without uttering a word.

I was afraid, and my knees trembled.

One afternoon, in the middle of one of their fights, I squeezed Tránsito's hand, and she took me to see the hive the bees were making under a plank of the canoe.

Tránsito kept insisting on returning to the islands, and I asked her if she'd forgotten how hard it was for us to come to the city. I reminded her that when we came here, I was twelve years old and she was seventeen, and a man at the dock told us we didn't have enough money to pay for the ferry, so we got in a canoe and rowed all day long. We let the current carry us, afraid our canoe would get sucked in by a whirlpool. We kept rowing the entire trip, without hearing a thing but the sound of water or the screech of an owl.

Tránsito listened to me, as if I were talking about a journey she hadn't made. She told me she remembered arriving here and that she couldn't forget the lights of the city off in the distance.

Tránsito, I want to tell you something, I told her.

She looked at me impatiently and said,

Not now.

At that moment, Ortiz arrived with help, and we headed back.

The Ford Falcon climbs the winding driveway leading to the house, then turns onto the side road to the servants' quarters.

Tránsito says to Lucía,

I can't wait to get home and stick my feet in a tub of cold water.

Stop your complaining and sighing, we're here.

Ortiz stops the car by the kitchen door to let the women out and drives the car to the back of the garden.

The Señora is waiting for them in the doorway and orders,

Make me a cup of tea, I'll be right there. Tránsito looks at Lucía and says,

Poor patrona . . .

Lucía interrupts her,

She seems fine to me.

They go into the kitchen, and Tránsito sits down in a chair, takes off her shoes, wiggles her toes, and feels needles jabbing the soles of her feet. She does not speak. She cannot forget that just a while ago, they were returning from the Señor's funeral, and while they waited in the car for Ortiz, Lucía told her that she was not going back to the islands with her, that she was staying.

It's so sticky, a storm's on the way, says the cook.
The servant responds,
I hope it gets here soon because I can't take it anymore.
Lucía screams at her,
That's what you get for living in sandals and wearing a pair of heels today of all days!
Don't yell at me, it's just that I never have time to get them stretched.

The shouts from the kitchen get louder and the chauffeur hears the women and stops what he is doing to see what is going on.

Tránsito tells Lucía that she sacrificed her whole life for her and now she is going to abandon her.

Lucía reacts with rage.

The house is closed up and dark. The servant opens the shutters while the cook and chauffeur go about their business. The scent of calla lilies and chrysanthemums lingers in the air.

Tránsito walks barefoot, letting the cold tiles relieve her aching feet.

She rearranges the chairs that had been left scattered about the living room, then goes to the window, and looks outside. The rain begins to fall, filling the air with the smell of damp earth, and as the weeping willows sway in the wind, the servant broods.

Lucía told me that she and Ortiz had bought the last plots left in the new section of the cemetery. I didn't speak. But I believed that it was clear to both of us that we wanted to return soon to live out the rest of our days together there, on the other side of the river, before our memories vanish for good; to die where Mother was buried, near the ravine, by the grove of *talas* and *espinillos*, where we took our first steps.

Lucía looked at me wide-eyed, stammered, and said,

I'm staying here, I've bought my grave. Go back yourself, if you want to.

My hands and legs trembled, and everything went black. I was so angry I couldn't say a word. Her voice sounded strange to me, as if it didn't belong to my sister. She told me what I never wanted to hear, and I was afraid.

While we were living on the island, Mother got together with Lucía's father. I never met mine, and that man was like a father to me. He fixed canoes and taught me how to patch boats. We'd cover the frame to strengthen it, fill the joints of the planks with hemp, and then coat everything with pitch and filler so the water couldn't get in. He learned the trade working at the shipyard in Ibicuy.

I remember his big hands sanding the *timbó* wood that had been pitted by the waves. He'd spit while he worked. I remember everything. Back then, time didn't matter to us.

Lucía's father isn't the same anymore. He doesn't speak to Mother and he screams at us over the slightest thing. Lucía and I don't understand the things my stepfather says about Mother and the men she has, and we don't understand what Mother says about the women he has either.

Every time I offer to help him, he yells at me to get out of the way.

The three women are dressed in black and sit at the table drinking tea, sipping it slowly, a little at a time. One of them is the wife of the deceased, the other the servant, and the third, the cook.

The widow's hands shake as she raises the teacup and says she cannot remember the last name of the commander who had the audacity to show up at the funeral.

I have it on the tip of my tongue . . . Was it Villalba or Banegas, that son of a bitch?

Drink your tea before it gets cold, and stop getting yourself all worked up, says the servant.

The Señora finishes her tea, stands up, picks up the cup, and goes over to the sink.

The cook stops her,

Where are you going?

Get out of my way.

The cook and the *patrona* struggle until the cup slips from her hands, falls to the floor, and shatters into bits and pieces.

Patrona, *look what you made me do!*

I'll take care of it. I'll have it swept up in a second, says the servant.

She gets the broom and sweeps the pieces of china scattered on the floor, picks them up with the dustpan, and throws them away.

Why don't you rest a bit, Señora? the cook suggests.

I'm going upstairs now.

I sweep up the pieces of china and throw them away.

Now I'm where I never thought I'd find myself. Lucía's going to stay with Ortiz. And the Señora and I . . .

I don't need much to survive.

The cook takes Ortiz a cup of coffee and in the hallway comes across Tránsito, who rushes past her.

I don't know what she's up to, coming and going like that. Her feet can't be hurting her that much . . .

Lucía sees Ortiz shining the car, as if he were going to take the Señor somewhere.

Drink your coffee before it gets cold, she tells him.

The chauffeur puts down the chamois cloth and thanks her.

He drinks it slowly, while she shifts back and forth with that rocking motion she has had ever since she can remember.

She returns to the kitchen and runs into Tránsito on the way.

What are you doing? she asks her.

She walks by and does not respond.

The cook thinks,

Maybe she needs help. I'm going upstairs.

Lucía sees that the *patrona*'s bedroom door is closed and opens it slowly. It is dark inside. She can barely see the Señora, resting in bed, with her eyes closed. She tiptoes over and looks at her, then sits down in the armchair and stays there, without making a sound, for some time.

Suddenly the door opens, Tránsito enters, panting from climbing the stairs, and upon seeing Lucía, whispers to her,

Shhh, don't make any noise, you'll wake her up. Let's go into the hallway.

Lucía says,

Where have you been, Tránsito?

You startled me.

What should we have for dinner?

You want me to help you?

You know I don't like you meddling in the kitchen.

And I don't like you sticking your nose in the Señora's bedroom.

Tránsito closes the door, and Lucía goes downstairs.

I'm going to make saffron rice. I already know the Señora will eat it without telling me she likes it, or she'll turn up her nose. She can't bring herself to say, *it's delicious*. After all these years, I still don't understand why she complains about my cooking and picks at it.

Nothing can please her.

I don't know what I'd do without Ortiz . . .

Why is it that some people have money and can't be satisfied and want more, but they don't realize that having more only causes more problems? And that's what I'll never understand about the Señora.

No doubt, as Tránsito says, the Señora had it all figured out. Before the Admiral died, she got him to tell her where he kept his mother's ring. That's the way she is, and there's nothing we can do about it . . .

Even so, I don't think she'll get used to living alone. I'm not that smart, but you don't have to be to realize that. The three of us won't get used to living without the Señor either.

And to think that at first he refused to bring us from the islands to work here, saying we were much too young to take care of the house.

The Admiral never liked girls. That's why he always said that he forgave his wife for not getting pregnant.

Tránsito says the *patrona* told her the truth, that it was the *patrón*'s fault they couldn't have children.

Just about everything the Señora says about me is because she hates people with dark skin, or mangy Indians, as they like to call us . . . If it hadn't been for the Señor, Tránsito, Ortiz, and I would have left this place a long time ago. The Señor treated us with respect, although who knows if he felt the same way she did, I shouldn't fool myself. Maybe he was good at hiding his feelings.

It hurts me a lot that the *patrona* feels that way. Sometimes it upsets me.

Ortiz is right when he says that I can't change her and that I should do whatever she orders me to without saying a word.

The servant goes to her room, looks for her bag, opens it, and puts in more clothes. She is tired and lies down while she thinks about having to cross the river again.

Something moved between my legs and pricked me. I stuck my hand in the mud and pulled out a catfish by its whiskers. I took it home in a bucket.

A few days later, I found it dead, floating in greasy water that smelled like gas. Lucía had sprayed it with insecticide.

Tránsito looks at the things around her, that have kept her company her for so many years: the iron bed, the armoire, the photograph of her mother.

Next year I'll come back and visit, God willing.

She thinks she hears voices in the hallway. Startled, she wonders about the Señora.

She's sleeping.

The thought calms her nerves.

The servant straightens her dress and goes into the bathroom. She gazes in the mirror and what she sees is not her reflection but that of another woman peering at her from the other side.

With the handle of her brush, she strikes the glass, and it breaks into shards that stay in place.

Confused, she looks at the shattered mirror again and sees the cracked face of the *patrona*.

What are you afraid of, Tránsito? Look at me, look up. I'm your patrona. *I'm happy, we're going to be friends, we're going to travel together, we'll keep each other company, always, always . . .*

How dare you say that to me now, after you abused me and treated me like a nobody? Like I was a beetle, a thing as dark and brown as a monkey? A shitty half-breed . . . No, Señora. No . . .

The servant rushes out of the bathroom, climbs the stairs, enters the Señora's bedroom again, and goes over to her bed,

You're not who you seem to be. Do you still want to keep tormenting me?

Go right ahead, but I'm not the Tránsito I used to be.

Look at your white hands . . . They don't lie. Betrayal begins with the hands, Señora. You know I'm leaving and I'm never coming back, and we'll see if I take you with me.

The servant airs out the room, opening the window after the downpour. She fluffs the pillows, puts away the Señora's shoes, hangs up her fur coat, and gets the mop and shines the floor. Then she collapses on the sofa, saying,

I always liked to do things perfectly. That's the way I am . . .
And she sits there staring into space.

Tránsito listens to the blustering wind, then goes to the window and looks at the clouds darkening the sky, and says to herself,

Those dust devils are going to dirty the house that I just cleaned. Oh well, I know there are worse things, but when it comes to dust, it never ends. You pass the feather duster, and it falls to the same spot. It's enough to wear you out.

Mother said that it was midday when she gave birth to me in the canoe. She used her teeth to cut the umbilical cord that joined me to her. I'd like to remember that moment when I came out of her body and peeked my head into the boat, but I can't.

I'm hungry.
I don't know where I'm going to sleep tonight . . .

I can't forget to bundle up the Señora before I leave. It's starting to get cool.
Soon I'll be near Mother again.

The old woman remembers when she was nine years old . . .

She's counting the buttons on her dress to see what the future will bring . . . *house, cottage, cabin, palace, chalet* . . .

As she looks for the saffron, Lucía thinks,

What if I talk to her about my sister . . . But this isn't the right time.

When we were kids, we made her steal melons. If only we'd known she'd make a habit of it!

A little while ago, she kicked me out like a dog, leaving me standing there like an idiot with that condolence telegram in my hand.

If I keep talking about Tránsito . . . Best to keep my mouth shut.

Could it be the Señora caught her red-handed again?

Like the Señora says whenever she gets angry, I really don't want to know.

That dimwit Lucía thought I didn't know what was going on.

I saw her leaving the laundry room with Ortiz more than once.

You can see everything from the little window that looks down on the patio.

What's gotten into Tránsito? She comes and goes, without taking a break, not even at a time like this. It makes me tired just watching her.

Then she complains about her aching bones.

She likes to be in charge and is downright uppity. If you ask me, that's why no man ever wanted to settle down with her.

Ever since the Señor got sick, the only thing she needs is the uniform, a cap, some shiny boots, and a few more pounds to be just like those women who guard the border in communist countries. That's what the Admiral once told me.

I think she's become more arrogant and conceited than ever. I can't stand her. She looks at me like I was a murderer. What did I ever do to her? Why did she throw me out like a dog just now when I took the Navy telegram to the Señora?

How ungrateful can you be? It's best I not mention this to Ortiz. It'll just add more fuel to the fire.

Ortiz is right: Tránsito has forgotten she's the servant. She wants to be like the Señora. She imitates her, speaking, walking, and moving like her. She's a ridiculous busybody.

It irks me that the Admiral's body isn't even cold yet and Tránsito's already bossing around the *patrona* and acting like she's a member of the family.

I don't know why the Señora can't see that . . .

The mechanic changes the fan belt, and the Ford starts up. When he finishes, the chauffeur pays him and the man leaves.

Ortiz gets into the Ford.

Wouldn't you know this would have to happen to us right here at the gate to the cemetery.

When one thing goes wrong, everything else does too, Tránsito responds.

The Señora must have arrived at the house by now, Lucía says.

I worry about leaving her alone, Tránsito adds.

For God's sake, step on it!

We'll have an accident, Lucía. Don't make me more nervous than I already am, and quit rattling that key. You know I can't stand to be rushed or told what to do.

We're almost there.

Ortiz makes a sharp turn and suddenly the river comes into view.

The two women say nothing. The chauffeur glances at them in the rearview mirror. The silence grows, and he does not speak either.

The chauffeur drinks his coffee slowly and looks at Lucía and tells her that it tastes good and strong.

He says softly,

You're just like your mother, even in the way you look, and when you do something, you do it perfectly or not at all. On the other hand, Tránsito . . .

Lucía smiles and returns to the kitchen.

Ortiz is shining the Ford, and when he goes to get the chamois cloth, he hears the doorbell ringing incessantly.

Doesn't anyone in this house hear that doorbell? Where in hell are the women?

The chauffeur goes to open the door. The mailman is there and hands him a telegram.

Ortiz says to Lucía,

Another message of condolence for the Señora. Will you take it to her?

Yes.

As Lucía makes the Señora the cup of tea she just requested, she shouts at Tránsito,

How could you step in front of the patrona *as they lowered
the coffin? What were you thinking, that you were the dead
man's wife?*

*We lived more years with them than Mother. I feel like this
house is mine, and the Señora told me I was part of the family.
You're jealous, aren't you?*

*Don't yell at me, Tránsito. I've had it with you. You're so
confused.*

Lucía explodes,

I can't take it anymore.

At that moment, Ortiz walks in and tells them to stop argu-
ing over stupid things and let the *patrona* rest.

Show a little respect.

It is almost midnight. The servant stands by the window of the Señora's bedroom, wondering,

What if I take her with me?

She turns around, looks at the dead woman and tells her,

Get up. We're leaving.

Tránsito goes to the armoire, takes out a flowered dress and shoes made of the same fabric, and places them on the bed.

Get dressed. Hurry up. We don't have much time.

You're not coming with me like that, without any makeup.
I'm going to make you pretty . . .

Tránsito gets the Señora's cosmetic bag, takes out the *Angel Face* powder and brush, and dusts her cheeks and chin.

She puts lipstick on her, then goes to the dresser and finds the hand mirror under the *patrona's* black veil, and holds it up to her face,

Can you see the difference? You're a new woman. That helps. It's a start.

At first the woods are spooky, but after awhile you'll get used to them. After I teach you to scare away the bees with smoke so you can get the honey from the beehive, you're going to like living on the other shore, and after a few months, you won't even remember this house.

I know this will be good for you, because you're just pretending, you're not really dead.

The servant struggles to lift the Señora, but the body is too heavy and falls over. She pulls it to the floor, grabs one arm of the cadaver, and drags it toward the staircase. She pushes the body, and it rolls down several steps, making a thud that can be heard downstairs.

Is that you, Tránsito?

She sees a light in Lucía's room.

Tránsito quickly gets her purse and bag and leaves. She walks in the darkness toward the riverbank and goes down the few steps leading to the dock. When she hears Lucía calling Ortiz, she realizes there is no time to go back for the Señora. A cold, intense fear comes over her.

The wind changes direction and then everything falls silent.

The old woman carries a bag in one hand, and in the other her purse. She walks quickly, her legs and hands trembling. She leaves the house through the service door.

Lucía's shouts echo through the house and garden.

Tránsito, Ortiz, help me, the Señora fell down the stairs and she's not moving. Hurry!

The old woman quickens her pace. She takes off her shoes and walks on the sand to the pier, where the canoes are tied, and murmurs,

She's dead.

She gets in a canoe, places the bag and purse on the seat, unties the rope from the pier, and as she curls up on the floor, the boat begins to drift away. She hears the water hitting the *timbó* wood, and as in her childhood, she thinks the waves are singing: *échale caá, échale caá, échale caá. Guarumba Taitá, Guarumba Ahuevé, échale caá, échale caá, échale caá* . . .

She rolls on her side and makes certain the little gray bag with the ring inside is around her neck, then she curls up tightly and before falling asleep, whispers,

Mother, I'm coming now. Wait till you see the gifts I have for you!

APRIL 7, 1979

Yesterday afternoon, I saw the *patrón* in his bed for the last time. For a moment, he looked toward the window, his eyes shifting back and forth as if waiting for someone who hasn't arrived.

Then he shouted,

What the hell is the fleet doing there?

It was the last thing he said.

Then he closed his eyes and didn't speak again.

A little later, Tránsito came in, and I left.

Once again I hear the sound of the water breaking against the ship and the *patrón* asking me to take care of the pheasants while he's away. He says he'll return before winter and says goodbye with a pat on the back and walks toward the ship. I can imagine him now, greeting the crew as the ship slips away into the fog, and a Navy vessel follows not far behind.

May God protect you, Admiral.

The chauffeur finishes polishing the Ford and recalls the day when he was driving the Admiral to the border, and he told him about Captain Villegas. He said he was a traitor, that he was full of shit, and he wanted to stomp on his head.

The Admiral needed to get rid of him, and Ortiz remembers when he asked him to handle that. Afterwards, he got sick and never mentioned it again.

A little while ago, when he saw Villegas at the *patrón's* funeral, Ortiz wondered what that son of a bitch was doing there and noticed how old he looked . . .

The chauffeur went over to him anyway and offered his services, and immediately Villegas responded that he should come and see him.

Ortiz smiled.

The chauffeur could wait for his boss for hours. He would go to a bar, order a cup of coffee, smoke a cigarette, and sit there watching a game of pool.

He did not like to talk to strangers about his job. He preferred to be alone.

Once in a while, when they would invite him to play poker, he would accept. He was always bad at cards. Then he would leave to get some air and kill time.

He would stretch his legs, walk a bit, and after a while, pick up the Admiral. Then he would have to drive back before the sun came up, staring ahead with his eyes wide open.

The Ford goes down a road flanked by vineyards and cotton-wood trees. It is the first time the chauffeur has seen the mountain range with its snowy peaks.

He tells the Admiral that he wishes they could cross the border.

What do you want us to do, Ortiz, fly?

Do you think it's that bad, Admiral?

Don't be a pussy, Ortiz. The road to the border is mined. We're going to smash those sons of bitches! If they want war, that's what we're going to give them. The islands and the Beagle belong to us.

Those shitty Chileans will see what we Argentines are made of.

They left the hotel in Cacheuta as the sun was coming up. The cold stung their faces. As they got into the Ford, the Admiral said,

You know something, Ortiz?

What, Admiral?

We never quit: when we're not wiping things clean inside, we have to clean them up outside.

How much further to the border, Ortiz?
We still have a way to go. Rest, Admiral.
They're threatening us, Ortiz. They need to understand
when they've crossed the line. We're going to wipe them out.

The Admiral was hot-blooded and would lose control quickly. I'm not like that, I'm good at waiting; that's my nature, but inside things take their natural course. I learned that as a boy, working in the shipyard at Ibicuy.

Now I can work wherever I want, even for Captain Villegas.
Lucía says that when I retire I'm going to have time to do other things, but I can't sit still. Wasting time isn't for me.
I'm satisfied with what I do.

The law was always after my father. On the island they said that he'd stabbed a guy.

I never looked for him or heard any more about him. I never knew if they caught him, or if, as some said, he crossed the border into Paraguay or Brazil.

My mother was the one who cried over him until the day she died.

She waited for him. She waited for him her entire life.

I don't know why I remember that, at this very moment . . .

The only image I have of my father is when he called me to help him hold down the pig he was about to butcher.

Now that the Admiral's gone, I bet the Señora will let Lucía and me go and keep only Tránsito. Even if it costs her a bundle.

I can hear her now,

This is for Lucía and for you. Come back and get the rest next month . . .

But she better pay me all at once. She's not going to screw me.

CAST

Tránsito, the Servant
Lucía, the Cook
Ortíz, the Chauffeur
The Señora, the Admiral's wife

ABOUT THE AUTHOR

Perla Suez is an Argentine novelist, essayist, translator, and author of children's books. She was born in Córdoba but lived the first fifteen years of her life in Basavilbaso in the province of Entre Ríos. She has most recently been awarded the Permio Nacional de Novela, the most prestigious award that can be bestowed upon an Argentine author.

ABOUT THE TRANSLATOR

Rhonda Dahl Buchanan is a professor of Spanish and director of Latin American and Latino Studies at the University of Louisville. Her many translations include Perla Suez's *The Enter Ríos Trilogy: Three Novels*.